CN00406121

CLOSURE

Short Stories

Louise Braithwaite

For George

Contents

The Full Three-Sixty

So, as care homes go, this isn't such a bad one. Ultra-modern, and fairly self-contained; almost like being in sheltered flat, but with the bonus of round-the-clock care. There's a telly lounge, for those who want it, but most don't bother – we've all got them in our rooms. A smaller lounge for visitors, and they put activities on, most days; some good, some not so much, but there's no pressure to join in. For so long, I'd dreaded ending up somewhere like this, but now I'm here, it's fine – I'm actually quite enjoying it!

There are some lovely people in here, too, which makes all the difference. Admittedly, there's a couple I'd never have got along with in years gone by – macho men, back in the day, but even *they're* alright. Mellowed with age, no doubt. It's weird, though. Looking at us, you can tell we're elderly; frail, even. I mean, I've not long turned 86 (just *wrong*, on every level!), and one lady's nearly 100! And yet, none of us act or dress "old" at all. Or at least, not like old people *we* remember! We've all got our laptops, or tablets, or i-phones, and we're all on social media. Even the 99-year-old is on Facebook!

Most of us miss getting out, so they try their best to bring that to us. There's a proper restaurant with a bar – a decent menu with specials every night, and a choice of wine (not the *best* wine I've ever tasted, but you can't have everything!); and that's where I noticed him, that first night, next table along.

It sounds mad to say he hasn't changed. I last saw him in 1970 – that's *68 years*!! We were still in our teens at the time, I remind myself, in the hope it might even *slightly* soften the blow (it doesn't come close). Unbelievably, his hair is still a reddish, sandy light brown – a few streaks of white, but nowhere near what you'd expect. Slender, elegant – some lines, of course, but he *still* has those cheekbones! It took a while for him to recognise me, but no surprise there. I was in two minds whether to let on –after all, we didn't part on the best of terms – but in the end, it was him who spoke to me.

"Excuse me - I could be completely wrong, but I'm sure I know you from somewhere. I just can't put a name to the face."

"Yeah," I said. "It's been a long time, but you'd be right. It's Chris."

"*Chris*?" He frowned. "Sorry – it's just, I've worked with a few Chrises, over the years, and you don't look like any of them."

I shook my head. "When I say a long time, I mean a *really* long time. Chris Harper. From high school?"

"Oh!" His face dropped slightly (I'm used to that!) "Oh! …I see… so now you're… you've…"

"No," I said lightly. "I'm still a guy. I've lived as a woman for 40-odd years, but I never made the change."

Before I could say any more, a nurse was whizzing him off to the small lounge.

"You've got a visitor, Stuart – your friend Kay."

I notice she comes quite often, this friend – once, maybe twice a week, sometimes with her husband (Phil, I think); a red-haired woman and a bearded man. There's another couple, too – Jill and Rachel? – one flamboyant, the other classy and restrained. They all seem in their 60s, maybe early 70s, but it's hard to tell - no-one really looks their age, these days.

It's been almost three weeks since we spoke; I see him most nights in the restaurant, but he's always at the other end of the room. I was starting to feel a bit paranoid, wondering if he'd asked them to keep me away; but now, today, they've sat us together for Sunday lunch. It's Mother's Day, and pretty quiet in here, with most of the ladies out to lunch with their families – so we get the table to ourselves.

It's more than a little awkward at first. As we eat in silence, he plays anxiously with his food (a habit he had way back) and clears his throat a few times.

"Look, Stu," I say at last. "If you'd rather I sat somewhere else, just let me know. I can ask the nurse to move me."

"No! No - of course not! It's just…" He sighs. "To be honest, Chris, I'm glad of the chance to speak to you. I know it was years ago, but I've always felt terrible about how things ended between us, on that last day of school. You were such a great friend to me, and the way I brushed you off… It was unforgiveable."

He's not the only one to feel bad. Things had already been tough for him at that school, and no doubt he was confused enough, without…. Let's just say, I completely understood why he'd want to get as far away as possible. He couldn't have been angrier than I was – at *me*.

It felt right at the time. I *know* that's a cliché, and what we all say when we've messed up, but it was true. We were so close. Unlikely friends, on the surface. I was loud, in-your-face (still am!), and didn't take being bullied lying down. He was shy, aloof, stoic, and took it all in stony silence. I admired that in him; always felt they got more of a rise out of me. Mum and Dad never found out about the bullying till years later, and I know it shocked them – because this wasn't an inner-city comp, it was a "posh" boys' grammar school in a leafy suburb.

Now, just to be clear, I've got nothing against Formby – it's a beautiful place. When we moved, Mum had just gone back to teaching, and Dad had been promoted to Deputy Head. I don't blame them for wanting a bigger house, and I think they chose Formby for the beach. But, for those who don't know Liverpool, the north end is less diverse than the south, and that was the whole trouble. I lived in Wavertree until I was 12 – not a million miles away from Toxteth, where Mum grew up, towards the top of Smithdown Road by Lodge Lane. She was half-African, half-Chinese; my grandad was a seaman from Sierra Leone, and my nan's family ran a laundry on Pitt Street. And back then… I'm not saying things are perfect now, by any means – still plenty of racists knocking about, but at least it's not *acceptable* these days, like it still was in the 60s.

Despite missing my old friends, I loved our new house at first. It had a huge garden with apple and laburnum trees, in a lush green setting near the sea. The neighbours were lovely, too – overwhelmingly white, course, but always friendly. Just a pity the same couldn't be said for the school.

The bullying was never physical – just ridicule and exclusion, which was bad enough, although at least easier to hide from my parents. Being white and middle-class was a huge part of fitting in, which went without saying; and by middle-class, I mean a traditional, right-wing, very Protestant middle-class, worlds away from my bohemian parents and their friends. But it wasn't just that – you also needed a certain personality. Driven, competitive, extrovert; good at sport, and it helped if you preferred science over art. I guess I ticked the "extrovert" box, but safe to say, my style of extroversion was nothing like theirs.

Stu, at first glance, was a little better-off. White, straight-acting, and from a family far more conventional than mine. Brilliant at chess and debating, and with that, I suppose, he did have a competitive streak. But at the same time, an extreme introvert who loathed sport; and although he did quite well at Maths and science, his passion was for the arts. None of this went down well – and then he palled-up with me!

Of course, they all assumed that Snowe and Harper were an item. I won't lie when I say I'd have *loved* that to be true! But, in reality, I didn't know if Stu was even gay. I suspected he was, but he always played his cards so close to his chest... He was just a really dear friend – and despite hating everything about that school, I was happy there because of *him*. Any feelings I had for him, I was wise enough to keep to myself – until that last day.

It was an exciting time – and all I can think is that I must have been caught up in the euphoria of leaving. We both had places at Uni lined up – he was going to art school in Glasgow, I'd be doing music at Leeds. And best of all, we'd never have to set foot in that hell-hole again! All I know is that I hadn't *planned* to kiss him; but it happened and, to begin with, it felt completely natural, and as though it was right for him, too. But then it went deeper, and he pulled sharply away.

"Just... just leave me alone!" His voice was shaky, and he looked on the verge of tears. "I don't... I'm not... You've got it all wrong! It's best we don't keep in touch."

Several decades and two marriages later, and it still feels like a kick in the face. But I can't tell him that – he clearly feels bad enough already, and what would be the point?

"You know, there's been plenty of water under the bridge since then," I say steadily. "No doubt we've both changed a lot – and besides, it was *me* who was at fault, for assuming you felt the same."

Stu shook his head. "But that's just it, Chris – I *did* feel the same!"

Ridiculous, really – the lift that gives me, almost 70 years on.

"It took me years to come out," he continues. "Even longer before I told my family. It didn't go down well, but there was some relief in getting it over with, I suppose. I married a girl from art college in my 20s – convinced that if I could make it work, perhaps I *wasn't* gay, after all.

"It lasted five years. Her name was Lydia. Very quiet and withdrawn – even more than I was. Looking back, our parents pushed us into marriage – hers were worried about her being so shy, and that she'd never meet anyone. Mine were the same, I guess, although a bit less vocal about it. In some respects, it did us good – especially her. Although her family meant well, they could be very over-powering; and once she'd got away from them, she really seemed to blossom.

"Trouble was, the more she came out of herself, the more she wanted from the marriage. She'd been terrified of sex at first, which suited me fine, but as things began to change... The Snow King, she used to call me. Partly because of my name, of course, but mainly because I never went near her. I don't blame her for feeling resentful – after years of blending into the background, she wanted to feel desirable. She found someone else, in the end; and although I still cared for her, I can't say I wasn't relieved.

"A year or so after it ended, I met Julian Forrest – the love of my life. We were both teaching at school in Southport – he was very loud; very funny – not so different to you. We were together for nine years, but I *still* wasn't ready to come out, and that's what broke us up. He was sick of feeling like a dirty secret, he said – and although that was the last thing I intended, I understood. He wanted us to live together – to be a proper couple -and I couldn't have kept that from the family. The final straw was when my mother dropped in unexpectedly – Jules was there, and in panic, I pretended he was just a colleague. It felt so cold, he said – so clinical - and he couldn't carry on like that.

"It took years to get over Jules, and it was a long time before I ever bothered again; I honestly thought life was simpler alone. As I got into my 40s, Mum kept on and on at me, about why I'd never re-married. She knew Lydia had let me down, but not all women were the same, and why didn't I try again – maybe join a dating agency? She pushed and pushed, until one day I lost my temper and just blurted it out. Dad barely spoke to me after that – while Mum told me I was just confused, and blamed Lydia for putting me off women! I gave up trying to explain, after a while – and although it was hurtful, I can't say any of it was a shock."

He pauses – and although this was all at least 40 years ago, I can tell it still feels raw, especially how things ended with Jules.

"I'm sorry you went through that, Stu," is all I can say. "I feel quite guilty."

He laughs. "Whatever for?"

"Well – for how easy *my* life was, I suppose. Not that it's *all* been plain sailing, but at least my family were on-side. I'm very lucky."

"No – you weren't lucky, Chris, because that's how it *should* be. Nothing to feel bad for. And as for me – life could have been much worse, you know. I always did like my own company - and I used it as a time to focus on my writing."

"Do you still do your poetry?" I ask him.

"Yeah," he smiles, "I've self-published a few volumes, over the years. Didn't sell brilliantly, but then poetry generally doesn't."

"Still an achievement, though. That's great, Stu. Good on you."

"Thanks - it's something to just get it *out* there, isn't it? So…. As I said, after Jules it was many years before I met someone else, and when I did…" He clouds over, and again, I can tell that whatever it is, time hadn't made it easier.

"You don't have to tell me, you know," I say, "if it's too difficult."

"No… it's not *difficult*, exactly, just…. After 20 years, I still feel a complete fool. His name was Dominic, and he was younger than me – and by that, I mean *much* younger. There was a lot that reminded me of Jules – and you. Very outgoing, full of energy; made me laugh all the time. He'd trained as an actor, but his real talent was for comedy, and I'd really hoped he'd get to the Edinburgh Fringe. I met him through my friend, Rachel – you may have seen her visit sometimes."

"The lady who looks like Stevie Nicks?"

"Yeah – that's the one! So, I'd got my Headship by this time, and Rach's partner Jill was working for me at a primary school in West Derby – but I'd already been friends with Rach for years before that, right back to when she first started teaching. Dom had known her since his teens – he'd gone to a drama group she ran. He was in his late 20s by the time I met him, but they were still close. He'd had a troubled childhood, Rach said, and she always looked out for him – mothered him, even.

"Perhaps that was it – because *she* saw no wrong in him, I fell into the same trap of making excuses. It took a while, but in the end, I saw he was *nothing* like Jules; nothing like you. No kindness – no generosity of spirit. He got away with it because he was funny, but *his* funny was light years away from Jules'. Where Jules had a sense of the ridiculous, Dom liked to *make* people ridiculous. The put-downs and belittlement were constant. I kept convincing myself I was wrong, or imagining it. After all, most would take one look at us and say I was lucky to have him – that I was punching well above my weight! But it all came to a head in the end – when my friends Kay and Phil renewed their vows."

"The other couple who come here?"

"That's right. As it turned out, they weren't over-keen on having Dom along in the first place – they knew what he could be like, but couldn't very well leave him out if they wanted to ask me. Anyway, he decided to pick a fight, for no reason at all – just because he felt like. It was something he always did, whenever *he* wasn't getting the attention. Then, when it didn't go his way, he expected me to back him up. I wouldn't. I was furious, because I'd specifically asked him not to start anything, this time. He *knew* how much my friendship with Kay meant, but still wouldn't rein it in. So, I dumped him – right there, in front of everyone."

"Way to go!" I laugh. "I bet his face was a picture!"

"Of course, he tried to turn it round, and make out *he* was the one ending it. But the sucker-punch came when Rach had a go at him. He'd just taken it for granted that she'd be on his side, but she really ripped into him, and he ended up running off in tears. No-one heard from him again, or knew what became of him. It would be nice to think he learnt some life-lessons along the way – but sadly, I don't hold out much hope."

"Well, that's a narc for you," I say. "I've known enough of them in my time."

"Sorry to hear that, Chris. They drain the life out of you!"

"You're telling me!"

"I hope all came good in the end?"

I shrug. "Ups and downs, Stu, but you know me – that's how I like it! Worst point was back in '21, when I nearly died of COVID. It was touch and go for a while, and it took months to get on my feet. I wouldn't mind, it was just days before I was due for the vaccine! I'd known loads who got it who were fine, but I'd had pleurisy a few years before, and I guess that left a weakness. But, hey-ho! I'm still here, and plenty weren't so lucky."

"Dark days, indeed," he mutters. "I knew a few who didn't make it. My sister was one of them."

"That's rough, Stu. I'm sorry."

"Well, as you'll remember, she was a good bit older than me, and she did have some underlying conditions. I was half-expecting it, to be honest, but it's always a shock."

"That's true. I mean, my mum was 95 when she passed. I still can't believe it!"

"Same when mine went, for all our differences. It's never easy. But still..." He smiles warmly. "Here we are. And whoever would have thought we'd come full circle like this? It's so good to see you, Chris. I've missed you."

Closure

They were just looking out for her, they said. They knew how much she missed her Nanna, but she had to stop with all this nonsense – it was doing no-one any good.

"It's not nonsense!" she'd shouted. "And I'm not making it up about seeing her!"

Her dad sighed. "Look, darling - you really can't go on like this."

"That's right," her mum added. "So - I know you won't like this, sweetheart, but it might be for the best if you saw a doctor…."

"No way! There's nothing wrong with me!"

"Now, come on – no-one's saying there is…"

"Not in so many words," she said bitterly, as she stood to leave the table. "I'm going out."

"Oh, love - don't be like that! And you haven't even finished your breakfast."

"I've lost my appetite."

She'd taken Rusty for a walk along Otterspool Prom. They lived nearby, off Aigburth Vale, so this was something she did most Sundays - but today was much earlier, and much further. Anything to be away from *them*. They meant well, but they didn't have a clue – never had. Not like her Nanna; but then, no-one ever believed *her*, either…. She'd hoped the walk would calm her nerves, but the longer it went on, the more fired-up she seemed to get. Eventually, reaching the Albert Dock, she decided to stop off for an al-fresco coffee at Reuben's; perhaps that would give her the chance to collect her thoughts.

Being still early, Reuben's seemed fairly quiet – a few were sitting indoors, but outside on the terrace there was just herself and a fair-haired, bearded, middle-aged man in a naval uniform, who looked as despondent as she felt. Not eating or drinking, she noted; just staring off into space, seemingly unaware of anyone around him.

"Hi," she said at last. "Tell me to mind my own business, if you like – but is everything okay?"

As he turned, she saw his eyes were a beautiful, deep shade of blue-green, somewhere between jade and turquoise; and despite his forlorn demeanour, he was smiling.

"Thanks for asking, love," he replied. "And I'd never dream of being so rude." A deep, serious voice, with a slightly lilting, almost sing-song version of a local accent. "I'm okay, thanks. Well – that's to say, as good as I can be, under the circumstances."

Although she had no idea what these "circumstances" might be, she had an odd feeling that, deep down, she knew what he meant; and where he may have come from. She could be way off-beam, of course, but she'd stay and chat a bit more – see if her hunch was right...

"Look," she said, "if there's anything I can do to help – I mean, can I at least get you a coffee?"

"I'm fine, honestly – but thanks for thinking of me. It's very kind."

"No problems. I'm Trina, by the way."

"Bob. Nice to meet you."

Then a moment's silence, as she finished her drink, and he continued to look wistfully around him.

"Can't believe how much this place has changed," he said. "It was all derelict, when I was here last. 1977, that was."

Thirty-seven years. He looked nowhere near old enough – early 40s, at most.

"So," she asked, "you don't live in Liverpool, then?"

"I did, many moons ago. Dingle, born and bred. The Welsh Streets."

"Isn't that where Ringo Starr was born?"

"That's right – Madryn Street. We were in Voelas Street – we lived with my Gran, and it was the house my mum was born in. Quite nice houses, when they were first built. As well as having Welsh names, mostly Welsh people lived there – well, not so much in my day, but certainly my grandparents'. They'd come from a village called Mostyn - along the North Wales coast, not far from Rhyl. It's where my dad was from, too. But, as I said, that was years ago, and these days…. Well, let's just say, I move around a bit."

"I guess you'd travel a lot, in your line of work."

"No, no – it's a long time since I left the navy."

"Oh, right! I just thought…"

"I know." He laughed. "It must seem strange that I go around dressed in the uniform. You probably think I'm a bit of an oddball – but it was a happy time in my life, and…I don't know… it just seems to bring comfort."

"It doesn't seem strange at all," she said kindly. "Makes perfect sense to me. So – I guess it must feel weird, being back in Liverpool after all this time?"

"Not really. Because although I've not *lived* here, exactly, I'm often about. Always popping back and forth."

"I see," she grinned. "Can't stay away from the place, eh?"

"Yeah – that's one way of putting it. It's just *here* I've avoided. I know it's a famous landmark, these days, but it doesn't hold great memories." He sighed. "But time to face my demons, I suppose. I've been angry at my sister, Dot, for many years, and now… I don't think she's got much time left."

"Aw, that's so sad. I'm really sorry."

"Well – it is what it *is*, as they say. But what bothers me is, she's never known how I felt – and I'm just afraid it'll all come out when I see her. It'd be great to put it behind us and start with a clean slate, but I just can't seem to do it."

Start with a clean slate? That seemed such an odd thing to say, if the woman was about to die. Trina was beginning to get a sense of where this might be going....

"Has Dot been ill for a long time?"

"Yes – except, she doesn't know she's ill at all! Well, not in *that* way, anyhow. I mean, she's not been in good health for a while, but *she* thinks it's arthritis. She doesn't get around too well – the slightest thing seems to floor her, and I know it's something much worse that's causing it. Don't ask me *how* I know – I just do."

She didn't need to ask. Just like those horrible few weeks before she lost her Nanna, and that awful, sinking feeling of not being wrong.

"I'm like that, too," was all she said.

Bob smiled. "I can see that."

"So, what will you do? About Dot, I mean?"

"Forgive her, I hope. You know, it's not like what she did was even that bad – but it did hurt. She'd be devastated if I told her that, though."

"What was it?" Trina asked. "Sorry – I'm a nosy cow!"

"No, don't be daft! It's really helping, being able to talk like this. It's hard to put into words, really, because it's not just *one* thing." He sighed. "I suppose it all goes back to when we lost our mum. Well, that's to say, we didn't just *lose* her – she killed herself. I was 15 at the time – Dot was 13, and June, my youngest sister, just 10. But life was tough, even before that. I was always close to my dad – more so that Mum, I suppose – he was a lovely man, but hopeless with money. We lived in Woolton for a while, but they got heavily into debt, and we ended up back at Gran's.

"I guess we were lucky to have somewhere to go. But the trouble was, Gran had nothing down for Dad, and she was always on Mum's case, too – like it was her fault, for not keeping him in check. Mum was always highly-strung, and I think everything just wore her down. After she... after what happened, Gran never lost a chance to blame Dad, and he ended up hitting the bottle."

"That sounds horrendous, Bob." Talk about Captain Obvious! But what else could she say?

"Well," Bob continued, "if it was bad for me, you can imagine what it was like for the girls, being so young. June just went into herself, and Dot became a bag of nerves. I tried to protect them both, as best I could - but in hindsight, perhaps I was wrong for that. Dot started getting really clingy; not that I blame her, of course, but it didn't make things easy when I came to leave for the navy.

"I'd always wanted to go to sea. Dad encouraged me, but I kept putting it off for the girls' sakes – until, in the end, it reached a "now or never" point. Make sure you have no regrets, Dad kept saying, and when I saw how *his* life turned out, I guessed there had to be something in it. That didn't make it easier leaving Dot, though, and I'm not sure she ever completely forgave me. She'd write often, telling me how much she missed me, and how she couldn't wait till I was home. But when I *was* home, she'd do nothing but pick arguments, especially if I spent any time with June. I noticed her finding fault with everything June did – June was more confident by then, and Dot didn't seem to like that. The more it went on, the more I started to dread coming back at all!

"Still, I never stopped looking out for her. She was in her 20s when she started seeing DI Sam Stonehill – AKA the Laughing Policeman. His family had been neighbours of ours for years – his old man was long-dead by this time, but he'd been a nasty piece of work, and Sam was just like him. I could see he had Dot where he wanted her, but she turned on me when I tried to warn her off. I had no right interfering, she said – seeing as I left the first chance I got. And at the end of the day, *I* wasn't there for her, so could I blame her for turning to Sam? Look, sis, I said – it's not for me to tell you what to do. I'm just saying watch yourself, that's all. Well, she said, if you weren't away all the time, it might be different.

"Emotional blackmail. I can see now that's what it was, but at the time I was so worried, I gave it some thought. Then I met my wife, Viv, and that made up my mind.

"You'd think Dot would have been pleased when I left the navy. Perhaps she would have been, if it was just for *her* sake; but she couldn't stand Viv, and never exactly made a secret of it. Couldn't get her head around the idea I came home for them both; but then, that was par for the course with Dot. Always trying to make me choose between them.

"She used Viv's background as a reason to be against her – Viv's family were a bit rough-and-ready, you see. Her mum left them all for another bloke, and as for her dad…Good-hearted fella; would give you the shirt off his back if you needed it, but a law unto himself. In and out of jail for petty crime, and never seemed to learn. They'd always been what Gran called "dirt poor", and I think that's why he did it; out of desperation, more than anything else. I could only take as I found, and he always made me more than welcome – as did the rest of the family.

"Viv was 14 years younger than me – another thing for Dot not to like! Gran wasn't too happy, either. You do know that girl's just on the make? she'd say. She'd met her a few times before, because Viv worked in my Aunt Olive's florist shop. Olive was training her up, and she was really good – brilliant, in fact – but Gran thought she had ideas above her station. An upstart, she called her. Gran had helped Olive set up her business, and she seemed to think that gave her the right to stick her oar in. Much as we were grateful to Gran for taking us back in, she could be a real battle-axe - and I can safely say, the most judgemental person I've ever known. Dot had never met Viv until we got together. I guess she was influenced by Gran; although my gut feeling is, she'd have been like that anyway – whoever I was with.

"You seem to laugh more when *she*'s around, she'd say, and it always sounded like an accusation. God forbid, she might be *pleased* to see me happy! Perhaps she was right – I suppose I didn't laugh much with them, but quite honestly, there was nothing to laugh about! Whereas Viv was full of fun – really brought me out of myself. First time I met her, I'd popped into the shop while I was home on leave, just for a quick catch-up with Olive.

'This is my assistant, Viv,' Olive said. "You've not met her yet, have you?'

"No, I said, but I'd heard a lot about her.

"'All bad, I hope,' Viv winked. And it just went from there. Despite the age gap, and being so different in so many ways, we just seemed to click. We were married in less than a year – and as you can guess, it went down with Dot like a lead balloon!

"Of course, it had all ended with the Laughing Policeman by then. I had mixed feelings – because, as much as I didn't like the guy, or how he tried to run her life, I hated seeing her so unhappy. June was courting her husband Ray by then, and I was with Viv - poor Dot was left behind, and I really did feel for her. But we couldn't win. She kept pushing us away, then accuse us of not caring as soon as we backed off. Every time I saw her, there'd be some barbed comment about Viv; and of course, I was going to stick up for my wife! Whenever I did, Dot would say Viv was turning me against her. You're doing a good enough job of that yourself, I felt like saying, but managed to bite my tongue.

"I'll admit, I was relieved when she married Frank; perhaps now she had her own life, she might stop worrying so much about mine! Things did calm down a bit – she still made it clear she resented Viv, but at least Frank helped keep her grounded. Good, stand-up bloke, and he'd lost his mum at a young age too. His gran took them in, much like ours did; although I'm afraid to say, I've a feeling she was much nicer than ours! It was a happy marriage, although not without its problems, with their son Andy having Downs. There wasn't the same understanding, back in the 70s, and not everyone was kind.

"Viv and I were happy until my dad died – and that's when the depression hit. Looking back, I think it had been there all along, and just managed to keep it at bay. But losing Dad – I don't know... I think it brought everything home. Mum's death, the rows between Dad and Gran, all the stress when they lost the house in Woolton. Poor Viv did all she could to help me – but the trouble with depression is the way it makes you lie to yourself. I kept looking at Viv and thinking, what the hell's she doing with me? Someone else would snap her up in no time; and as hard as it might be, I'd be saving myself more heartache in the long run by ending it now.

"So, I told her to go. Said she could do better for herself, and although it might not seem like it now, I was giving her the best chance of happiness. She got so upset – said I *did* make her happy, and this was just a blip. But in my own head, I was convinced it was only a matter of time before she dumped me. Next thing – and it killed me to do this – I said I didn't love her anymore, and probably never really did. And we were totally wrong for each other – but that was my fault. I should have seen it from the start. Then she was in floods of tears....and I don't blame me if you're judging me right now, Trina. All I can say is, at that moment, I honestly believed I was doing the best for *her*.

"I told her I was sorry I'd hurt her. She wasn't hurt, she said, because she wasn't buying into it. She knew I was ill, and not thinking straight, and *that*'s why she was upset. She'd never believe I'd stopped loving her. But, if I needed space, she'd go and stay with her sister Rita for a while – give me a chance to feel better.

"Then she was gone – and of course, as soon as she was out the door, I knew I'd made the biggest mistake of my life. I'll give it a few days, I thought, then go round to Rita's to sort things out – but I was too much of a coward. No doubt, she'd have told Rita everything, and she'd have convinced her to have nothing more to do with me. No – I'd screwed up, big time, and I was going to have to live with it.

"But it was Dot's reaction that pushed me over the edge. Whatever she thought of Viv, I'd hoped she'd be able to put it aside, for my sake, if nothing else – like I'd done for her when she broke up with Sam. But she made no effort to hide how glad she was, and she wouldn't believe me when I told her I was the one to end it.

'Oh, come on', she said, 'we all know what that girl's like. There's no need to keep protecting her. I hate to say I told you so, Bob, but I *knew* she'd let you down. You're well rid!'

"It would be unfair to blame Dot for what I did next. But I suppose I just wanted to feel like my family had my back; and now Dad was gone, and June and Ray had moved down south, Dot was really all I had. And for her to see me unhappy and be so *pleased* - maybe it's not how she meant it, but that's what came across, and I'd never felt so desolate.

"Once I left, I knew I couldn't face going home, so I just kept walking. It could have been hours – could have been days. Didn't really think about where I was going; just went with my instinct and ended up *here*. As I was saying before, this was all derelict in the 70s. There was no-one about - my first thought was to drown myself in the dock, but then, last minute, I changed my mind. It was late at night, by this time, maybe early hours of the morning, and I stripped off and waded out into the river. Swam for a bit, then just drifted, until…. There's no happy ending, here; but you knew that already, right?"

Trina nodded. "I think I knew straightaway – especially when you said how long since you'd been here. You don't look anywhere near old enough. And the uniform…."

He smiled. "I wore that for the funeral."

"I thought so. Whenever I see my Nanna, she's always in the dress she wore for *her* day. The more you told me, I worked it out – and I'm just so sorry, Bob, that life got so hard."

Bob shrugged. "So am I, love. Because I'll tell you one thing – I regretted it as soon as I passed over. In fact, it was before that. Just in those last few seconds, when I realised this was it – and I'd *thought* it was what I wanted, but when it comes down to it, and you know there's no going back; no-one to save you at the 11th hour…

"Would I go to Hell? I wondered. Because you grow up believing that's what happens when you kill yourself. For Mum's sake, I hoped it wasn't true – and now, I was about to find out. I suppose it is, in a way, but not like it's portrayed. No fire, no underground – I mean, you don't have a body anymore, so how can you feel physical pain? But when you leave before your time… it's just that feeling that you'll never settle, because all you can do is watch the torment it causes to others – people you'd never dream of hurting in your normal state of mind.

"They found me three days later, washed up ashore. Viv got the news first. She was completely devastated – she honestly thought we'd end up back together. It was so horrible, seeing her in such a state, and knowing there wasn't a damn thing I could do. As for Dot – even now, I don't think she's over it. A couple of years ago, she was in tears because her son-in-law broke a vase I got them as a wedding gift. Not on purpose, of course, and he felt terrible over it. 'I know it's not the end of the world', she said to my niece, 'but it was from your Uncle Bob. And I still can't believe he's not here...'

"When I first passed, I was worried she'd do the same as me - and I honestly think she might, if it wasn't for the kids. Depression runs in our family, you see, and Mum wasn't the first one to end her life. I hated myself for what she went through. But having said that, I couldn't forgive how she was on that last day; or the way she treated Viv at the funeral.

"You can just imagine what a tough day *that* was. Viv was at the front with Rita (and me, if she only knew). On the row behind was Dot and Frank, June and Ray – and I could hear Dot, chunnering away about Viv being there at all, and giving her daggers, every chance she got. Rita was this little tough nut, and as they all came out of the Crem, she asked Dot what the f*** she was staring at. Dot, for all she lives on her nerves, gave as good as she got.

"'I don't remember anyone inviting *you*. And as for *you*, lady!' She glared at Viv. 'You've got some nerve, showing up today! All this is your fault – walking out on him, the first chance you got.'

"Poor Viv could hardly speak for crying. 'Look, Dot,' she managed to say, 'I know what you think of me – always have – but Bob asked *me* to go. You've got to believe me!'

"But Dot didn't want to hear it. If Viv had any respect, she said, she'd get out now, and steer clear in the future.

"'Oh, don't worry, love,' Rita sneered, 'the further away from *you* lot, the better! Come on, girl – let's get out of here, before I deck her one!'

"Dot was bad-mouthing Viv for the whole of the wake, then back home, in front of the kids; and even now, she never misses a chance to slag her off. She was exactly the same with her daughter Katie's husband."

"The one who broke the vase?" Trina asked.

"Yeah. That was years later, mind – and to be fair, I think Dot had just about accepted him by then. Although," he laughed, "I don't think 'Vase-gate' did him any favours! He's a biker-type, covered in tattoos, and from what I can gather, he had a pretty tough childhood; and like with Viv, it gave Dot the perfect excuse to take against him.

"I remember the lead-up to the wedding. Poor Katie - she couldn't do right for doing wrong! She'd had a spa-weekend with her mates for her hen-do; Dot kept moaning about feeling left-out, so Katie arranged a family meal, just to include her. Anyway, Dot spent the night going on and on, about how she was making the biggest mistake of her life – just like Uncle Bob with that bloody Viv.

"I'm listening to all this, fuming – wishing I could shake some sense into her. And yet I'm sorry for her, at the same time. No-one would want the life she's had – on top of everything with Mum, she lost Andy when he was just 18, and I know that was at the back of how she was with Katie. And now, poor Frank's got dementia. I doubt he'll take it in when Dot passes, which is a kind of blessing, I suppose. But it's Katie I feel for the most. It's already breaking her heart, seeing her dad like that, and she'll be in bits at losing her mum, for all she drives her mad.

"The thing that worries me is that once Dot joins me, it might just take one comment to make me lose my rag. And if I end up telling her the part *she* played in what I did that day, well... I just couldn't hurt her like that..."

"...because, whatever happened between you, she's still your sister – and you don't just stop loving someone."

"Exactly!"

Trina smiled. "You know what I reckon? That once you see her, it'll all go out the window – you'll just be so glad to get together again."

"That's what I'm hoping." Bob sighed. "But will it really be that easy?"

"From what my Nanna tells me, yes – I think it will."

"You miss her a lot, don't you?"

She nodded, tearing up. "She was the same as me, so we always *got* each other. I don't mean to have a go at Mum and Dad – they're lovely, and I know they mean no harm, but they think anything to do with the other side is a load of tosh. No evidence, they say, and that's what matters to them most – especially Dad, being a scientist. So, you can imagine how lost I was without Nanna. There was a time I thought of … of doing what you did… And then, when I was at my lowest, I started seeing her. Just when I'd given up hope – when I'd started doubting what I'd always believed.

"It brings a lot of comfort, but I just wish I'd never told Mum and Dad. I should have known better, because they say it's all in my head – a way of dealing with grief – and this morning, they were on about sending me to a doctor. The trouble is, the more they say it, the more I start to wonder if I *am* mad? Perhaps Nanna's not there at all – and I'm just seeing what I want to see. I'm glad I met you today, Bob; I just hope I'm not imagining this, too."

"Okay," Bob said. "So, I might have left way before the internet, or smart phones, or anything like that, but I try to keep up as best I can. I know they have those ancestry sites, these days. If you ever get the chance, you should go on one of them and look me up. Robert Hywel Lloyd – born 1934, died 1977; married 1966, to Vivien McIlroy. I wouldn't mention it to your parents, though – just do it for your own sake, to stop you doubting yourself."

"I will, Bob – I promise."

"And I know I'm a fine one to talk, but you won't do anything daft?"

"No – all those thoughts went, once I started seeing Nanna."

"Glad to hear it."

"How did things go for Viv?" she asked – but before he got the chance to reply, a man had joined them at the table.

"Mind if I sit here, love?" he asked. She hadn't realised how busy the café had become….

"Sorry, Trina," Bob said hurriedly. "I'll need to get going. Hope we can catch up again, one day."

And he was gone. Such a shame; she'd have loved to arrange another meeting - maybe find out what became of Viv. But this was how it had to be. She knew the score.

"Good luck for next week, Bob," she said, under her breath. "Rest easy."

A Blessed Release

He recognised her voice at once. A tiny, stoic, middle-aged woman, many years widowed. Her name was Anastasia; known to all as Nancy, or simply as "Nin".

She'd been "Nin" for ten years or more. He knew her to be 51, but you'd put her at least in her 60s – and that was probably because she was one of those "wise women" his parents spoke of, full of remedies and common-sense advice (but never judgement), who came into their own at times of crisis. Of course, she *looked* older, too. Always dressed the same – black shawl, white apron – her face lined and weathered, doubtless from the hours she put in, rain or shine, on her fruit-and-veg stall. But that wasn't uncommon around here – where so many of the women were gnawed by poverty and work... constant, ceaseless work....

He'd known Nancy for 23 years - since 1915, when he'd first come to the parish – and he recalled that even then, in her late 20s, she'd seemed careworn. Her husband, Frank, had died at sea, then she'd lost her beloved parents within months of each other. The years that followed were no kinder. He'd buried three of her children – Vincent, in 1916, from rheumatic fever; Gerard, in 1920, from TB; and more recently, her daughter Mary Ann, who died suddenly and shockingly from a stroke. Mary-Ann's husband, Joe, had fallen apart, and Nancy had swiftly brought the family to live with her.

Difficult to imagine what this calm, placid, utterly selfless lady could possibly believe she'd done wrong; yet here they were….

….. "Forgive me, Father, for I have sinned."

Then a long pause – two or three minutes, at least. Perhaps she'd lost her nerve, as so many did.

"Are you still there, my love?" he asked at last.

"Yeah…I – I'm sorry," she stammered. "I… it's just…not easy, that's all – knowing where to start."

"Then take all the time you need," he said kindly.

"Thanks… Thanks, Father. There's so much I need to say, but I'm scared I'll feel even worse, because… well, if it's just there, in your head, you can pretend it's not *real*, can't you?" She sighed heavily. "So - there's no easy way to say this, but - what sort of woman hates her own son?" Another pause; shorter than the first, as she seemed to take in a deep breath – and when she spoke again, he caught the sob in her voice. "And now I've got that out, I… well, it's a relief, but at the same time, there's no going back now, is there? And what must you think of me, Father? What must *God* think?

"All I can say is, you've been our priest for years, and you *know* what our Tony's like. And no-one can say I didn't try – in fact, in some ways, I even think it's my fault, for spoiling him. I felt sorry for him, you see, because he didn't have a dad. Maybe *that's* why he acts up, I used to think. But then look at our little

Frankie and Teresa – just lost their mam, and they're nothing like *he* was. Not even close! But at the time I'd think, he's only got me and our girls – no fellas in the house, and maybe he needs that. So, I tried to make it up to him. 'You're too soft, Mam,' our girls used to say, and I knew they were right, but….

"Perhaps I just didn't want to see it. *Still* don't, if I'm honest. Even now, I'll think, *surely* there must be a good side, somewhere? And maybe I *was* too soft with him, but they was all brought up the same – do as you'd be done by. I said it to him the other week, and he laughed in my face! 'Here we go again, Ma…'

"He was always a bully. The other kids were terrified of him, and that still makes me ashamed. Tormented the life out of poor Sally Dempsey. 'Simple Sal,' they called her, but I don't think she is - it was just the life she had. Her Mam died last year, and I really feel for her – it was always just the two of them. Don't get me wrong, Ellen was a lovely woman – loved the bones of Sal – but she wouldn't let her play out, or nothing like that. So, poor Sal ended up scared of her own shadow, and she's like a recluse now. Hardly goes out the door. Don't get me wrong, our Tony wasn't the only one to give her a hard time, but he was the worst, by a long shot.

"They lived next-door-but-one in the court, and now they're on the same landing, four or five doors down. I remember this day, a couple of years back. I was passing by on my way to work, and Sal was at the door - bringing the milk in, I think, so I stopped to ask how her Mam was. Our Tony wasn't far behind me – don't forget, he was still at home then, before he married Lizzie – and as soon as Sal caught sight of him, her face dropped a mile. I could see the fear in her.

"'What was that daft cow staring at?' he asked me later. 'Giving me daggers, she was!'

"'Well,' I said, 'think back to how you treated her.'

"'I don't remember,' he said, and that's probably true. It was all in a day's work for him, after all.

"'*She* does though, son,' I said. He just smirked. I could have slapped him.

"You probably know this already, Father, but he's been inside a couple of times for assault. Always getting himself barred from the pubs, and I reckon he might hit Lizzie, too. Now, don't get me wrong – I can't say I've ever really liked the girl. I always thought was a gobby mare, but she's gone so quiet, these past few months... And, as much as it gets on my nerves, I'd rather hear her mouthing off, because at least then I'd know she was alright. And now there's a little 'un on the way. I should be made up for them, but I'll be honest, it terrifies me - the thought of *him* being a dad.

"Then I think of how much Mary-Ann loved them kids, and it doesn't seem fair. I keep wondering, why her and not Tony? - then feeling angry at God, for putting me through this – and that's what made me come today, Father. Because I *shouldn't* feel this way, should I? I should just accept that He has His reasons, but the more I try to understand *why* He'd do this... All I can think is, He must be punishing me. You see, I had a terrible time having Tony – nearly lost him – and when he's at his worst, I often wish I had. And maybe God saw this, and thought he'd teach me a lesson, by taking Mary-Ann.

"But if that's true, Father... then is He really the God I thought He was? God is Love – that's what we got told, growing up, and I never doubted it. But could a loving God be *that* cruel? Unless... there isn't a God at all. And I hate myself for thinking that – but right now, I'm struggling, Father. Really struggling."

He waited a few minutes, in case more was to come.

"Okay," he said at last. "You know, you're not alone in this. I'd say most people have their doubts, at some point. I know *I* do."

"Oh!"

"Oh, yes – and that goes for a lot of us. You'd be surprised!"

"I just thought... well, you don't expect..."

"Look – I'm speaking off-the-record, you understand? In fact, I shouldn't really be saying this at all – to anyone – but the fact is, I never *chose* to be a priest. It was a common thing for families in Ireland to send at least one son to the priesthood, or a daughter to a convent; and that's probably true of Liverpool, too. And for many of us – well, let's just say, it's not the path we'd have chosen for ourselves. Sure, that doesn't mean I haven't made the best of it – I've always enjoyed helping people, and I can honestly say I love the job. There's not many who are that lucky! It's just the rest of it – and to be fair, I don't think I'd have ever married anyway, but that's not the point. It's a lonely life, at times, and it always struck me as wrong - *odd* – to think that God would want that for us. And then there's the bigotry – the things people do to each other, in the name of religion, and I don't know… I really don't know…"

"You see, that's what I think, too," she said. "Everything you just said then – it's exactly what's in my head, all the time. Then I wonder, is it just me? Or are we all thinking the same, but haven't got the guts to say it? The trouble is, Father, I hate feeling like this – and I want God to be real, because life's hard enough as it is, and if there's *really* nothing, then – there doesn't seem much point."

"Or perhaps the 'something' is just not what we thought. You know, we're raised to believe in God as a *man* – sitting there, above us all, watching and controlling what we do. But there's one big problem with that – we all have free will, and if He's completely in charge, how does that work? For a while now, I've wondered if the Quakers might be onto something when they talk of God as a *light* that's in each of us. But I daren't say that aloud – this is my livelihood, after all. I only hope that doesn't sound too cynical."

"No. You're just trying to survive, like we all are."

"You seem very wise. Can I ask, do you read a lot?"

"Yeah," she said hesitantly. "When I get the chance. Only when there's time, though – when everything's done."

"You sound like you're apologizing."

"Well – I do feel guilty, because there's always *something* to do in the house – and there's times I'll put it off a bit, until I've finished a chapter. I always take a book to the stall, in case there's not much doing, and when it gets busy, I find I'm longing for the quiet times so I can read. I know that's wrong – I should be wanting to make *more*, not less! – and all for the sake of filling my head with make-believe. If I well-off, it might be different."

"I see. So, you're saying books are only for the rich – not ordinary folk like you. And that's what you truly believe?"

"No," she sighed. "If I'm honest, no, but ...I'm like you, you see – I question things, but I couldn't dare tell anyone. Everyone else seems happy to accept their lot, but I never was, even as a kid. I can remember being about 10 or 11, and getting told my Uncle John – Mam's brother – had died in the workhouse. Mam was heartbroken, especially when she got the certificate, and the cause of death was exhaustion! It started from then, I think – but it wasn't just about rich and poor.

"We had next to nothing, growing up, but life could have been a lot worse – at least we had a lovely Mam and Dad. Mam went out cleaning when Dad couldn't get work, and Dad used to muck in around the house. I'd watch them together and I'd know that was how it should be – and I'd wonder why other men couldn't be more like Dad.

"I'd see other kids, bringing the ale home, terrified of spilling a drop in case their dads belted them. Neighbours with black eyes because their fellas knocked them about – but it was like they didn't seem to care! Like it was *normal*... and then, when Mary-Ann died - now, don't get me wrong, Father, I think the world of Joe. He's a good man – but on the days he's not in work, he's just sat there, waiting for me to come in and get his dinner on. Some days – *most* days – I'm that worn-out, I can hardly think straight! I know that's how life was for Mary-Ann, too, but she wasn't as strong as me – always sick as a kid, and I don't reckon she got over that. And I'm not saying it's Joe's fault, what happened, but.... It just doesn't seem fair that it's all on the woman, no matter what, and it winds me up that no-one else can see it.

"Anyway – I started a cleaning job a few months back. Just on a Wednesday morning - apart from Sunday, of course, it's the only day I close the stall. It's a Jewish lady I clean for – Leah Adler, her name is - about my age, maybe a bit younger. Clever woman - teaches at the university, and she lives near there too, in a flat on Hope Street. Bit of a long walk, but I've got a cousin who lives off Brownlow Hill, so I pop in on the way home. It's a day I look forward to.

"Leah's sometimes home when I'm there. She's become more like a friend, and that's not me being over-familiar – she says the same thing. We can talk for hours – *proper* talk, not just jangling. And when I tell her these thoughts, she gets what I mean – doesn't think I'm mad, like some would round here. She was a suffragette in her younger days, you see, and she reckons there's still a long way for women to go, even though it's better than it was. And – I don't know what you'll make of this, Father, I've never told anyone this, apart from her – but since I've been reading more, I've started writing poems. Leah helps me – she says I've got it in me to be really good. Perhaps she's just being kind, but all I know is, when I do it, I feel so much better. But then, like with the books, I start feeling guilty if I do too much – as if it's not really for the likes of me, and who do I think I am?

"I say this to Leah, and she gives me what-for – in a nice way! I've been through so much, she says, and *that*'s what writing's all about. And no-one's better than anyone! Since I've met her, I don't feel so lonely. Sounds mad, doesn't it? I mean, I'm with people all the time! But I can't talk to them the way I do with her. I know she's worried sick about what's going on in Germany, in case it starts happening here, and I'm scared for her, too – I may not have known her long, but I can't imagine life without her. I sometimes catch myself thinking of her, and... well, I won't say any more."

He knew what she meant, of course. It was the same with his dear friend and mentor, Father Declan Burke. Five years, since Declan had passed, and not a day where he wasn't on his mind.

"True friendship's never wrong," he said. "In fact, there's nothing wrong with *anything* you've told me here today. So, all this business of penance, and forgiveness – let's put it to one side, shall we? I just ask one thing – that you keep up the reading, and don't even think of giving up poetry!"

"I won't, Father, I promise." He heard her smile. "And thanks. Thanks so much!"

About the author:

Liverpool-based writer of "slice of life" fiction, set in and around the city.